'She was waiting,
but she didn't know
for what. She was
aware only of her
solitude, and of the
penetrating cold,
and of a greater
weight in the region
of her heart'

ALBERT CAMUS
Born 7 November 1913, Dréan, El Taref, French Algeria
Died 4 January 1960, Villeblevin, Bourgogne, France

All stories in *Exile and the Kingdom* published by
Penguin, 1958.

ALSO PUBLISHED BY PENGUIN BOOKS
The Outsider · *The Myth of Sisyphus* · *Caligula and Other Plays* ·
The Fastidious Assassins · *The Plague* · *The Fall* · *Exile and the
Kingdom* · *A Happy Death* · *The First Man* · *The Rebel*

ALBERT CAMUS

The Adulterous Woman

TRANSLATED BY JUSTIN O'BRIEN

PENGUIN BOOKS

PENGUIN CLASSICS

Published by the Penguin Group
Penguin Books Ltd, 80 Strand, London WC2R ORL, England
Penguin Group (USA) Inc., 375 Hudson Street, New York, New York 10014, USA
Penguin Group (Canada), 90 Eglinton Avenue East, Suite 700, Toronto, Ontario,
Canada M4P 2Y3 (a division of Pearson Penguin Canada Inc.)
Penguin Ireland, 25 St Stephen's Green, Dublin 2, Ireland (a division of Penguin Books Ltd)
Penguin Group (Australia), 250 Camberwell Road, Camberwell, Victoria 3124, Australia
(a division of Pearson Australia Group Pty Ltd)
Penguin Books India Pvt Ltd, 11 Community Centre, Panchsheel Park,
New Delhi – 110 017, India
Penguin Group (NZ), 67 Apollo Drive, Rosedale, North Shore 0632, New Zealand
(a division of Pearson New Zealand Ltd)
Penguin Books (South Africa) (Pty) Ltd, 24 Sturdee Avenue, Rosebank, Johannesburg 2196,
South Africa
Penguin Books Ltd, Registered Offices: 80 Strand, London WC2R ORL, England

www.penguin.com

Selected from *Exile and the Kingdom* published in Penguin Classics 2002
This selection published in Penguin Classics 2011
3

Copyright © the Estate of Albert Camus, 1958

All rights reserved

Typeset by Jouve (UK), Milton Keynes
Printed in England by Clays Ltd, St Ives plc

ISBN: 978-0-141-19584-1

www.greenpenguin.co.uk

Penguin Books is committed to a sustainable future
for our business, our readers and our planet.
The book in your hands is made from paper
certified by the Forest Stewardship Council.

Contents

The Adulterous Woman   1

The Silent Men   29

The Guest   49

The Adulterous Woman

A house fly had been circling for the last few minutes in the bus, though the windows were closed. An odd sight here, it had been silently flying back and forth on tired wings. Janine lost track of it, then saw it light on her husband's motionless hand. The weather was cold. The fly shuddered with each gust of sandy wind that scratched against the windows. In the meagre light of the winter morning, with a great fracas of sheet metal and axles, the vehicle was rolling, pitching, and making hardly any progress. Janine looked at her husband. With wisps of greying hair growing low on a narrow forehead, a broad nose, a flabby mouth, Marcel looked like a pouting faun. At each hollow in the roadway she felt him jostle against her. Then his heavy torso would slump back on his widespread legs and he would become inert again and absent, with vacant stare. Nothing about him seemed active but his thick hairless hands, made even shorter by the flannel underwear extending below his cuffs and covering his wrists. His hands were holding so tight to a little canvas suitcase set between his knees that they appeared not to feel the fly's halting progress.

Suddenly the wind was distinctly heard to howl and the gritty fog surrounding the bus became even thicker. The sand now struck the windows in packets as if hurled by invisible hands. The fly shook a chilled wing, flexed its legs, and took flight. The bus slowed and seemed on the point of stopping. But the wind apparently died down, the fog lifted slightly, and the vehicle resumed speed. Gaps of light opened up in the dust-drowned landscape. Two or three frail, whitened palm trees which seemed cut out of metal flashed into sight in the window only to disappear the next moment.

'What a country!' Marcel said.

The bus was full of Arabs pretending to sleep, shrouded in their burnouses. Some had folded their legs on the seat and swayed more than the others in the car's motion. Their silence and impassivity began to weigh upon Janine; it seemed to her as if she had been travelling for days with that mute escort. Yet the bus had left only at dawn from the end of the railroad line and for two hours in the cold morning it had been advancing on a stony, desolate plateau which, in the beginning at least, extended its straight lines all the way to reddish horizons. But the wind had risen and gradually swallowed up the vast expanse. From that moment on, the passengers had seen nothing more; one after another, they had ceased talking and were silently progressing in a sort of sleepless night, occasionally wiping their lips and eyes irritated by the sand that filtered into the car.

'Janine!' She gave a start at her husband's call. Once again she thought how ridiculous that name was for someone tall and sturdy like her. Marcel wanted to know where his sample-case was. With her foot she explored the empty space under the seat and encountered an object which she decided must be it. She could not stoop over without gasping somewhat. Yet in school she had won the first prize in gymnastics and hadn't known what it was to be winded. Was that so long ago? Twenty-five years. Twenty-five years were nothing, for it seemed to her only yesterday when she was hesitating between an independent life and marriage, just yesterday when she was thinking anxiously of the time she might be growing old alone. She was not alone and that law student who always wanted to be with her was now at her side. She had eventually accepted him although he was a little shorter than she and she didn't much like his eager, sharp laugh or his black protruding eyes. But she liked his courage in facing up to life, which he shared with all the French of this country. She also liked his crestfallen look when events or men failed to live up to his expectations. Above all, she liked being loved, and he had showered her with attentions. By so often making her aware that she existed for him he made her exist in reality. No, she was not alone . . .

The bus, with many loud honks, was ploughing its way through invisible obstacles. Inside the car, however, no one stirred. Janine suddenly felt someone staring at her and turned towards the seat across the aisle. He was not an Arab, and she was surprised not to have noticed him from the beginning. He was wearing the uniform of the French regiments of the Sahara and an unbleached linen cap above his tanned face, long and pointed like a jackal's. His grey eyes were examining her with a sort of glum disapproval, in a fixed stare. She suddenly blushed and turned back to her husband, who was still looking straight ahead in the fog and wind. She snuggled down in her coat. But she could still see the French soldier, long and thin, so thin in his fitted tunic that he seemed constructed of a dry, friable material, a mixture of sand and bone. Then it was that she saw the thin hands and burned faces of the Arabs in front of her and noticed that they seemed to have plenty of room, despite their ample garments, on the seat where she and her husband felt wedged in. She pulled her coat around her knees. Yet she wasn't so fat – tall and well-rounded rather, plump and still desirable, as she was well aware when men looked at her, with her rather childish face, her bright, naive eyes contrasting with this big body she knew to be warm and inviting.

No, nothing had happened as she had expected. When Marcel had wanted to take her along on his trip she had protested. For some time he had been thinking of this trip – since the end of the war, to be precise, when business had returned to normal. Before the war the small dry-goods business he had taken over from his parents on giving up his study of law had provided a fairly good living. On the coast the years of youth can be happy ones. But he didn't much like physical effort and very soon had given up taking her to the beaches. The little car took them out of town solely for the Sunday-afternoon ride. The rest of the time he preferred his shop full of multi-coloured piece-goods shaded by the arcades of this half-native, half-European quarter. Above the shop they lived in three rooms furnished with Arab hangings and furniture from the Galerie Barbès. They had not had children. The years had passed in the semi-darkness behind the half-closed shutters. Summer, the beaches, excursions, the mere sight of the sky were things of the past. Nothing seemed to interest Marcel but business. She felt she had discovered his true passion to be money, and, without

5

really knowing why, she didn't like that. After all, it was to her advantage. Far from being miserly, he was generous, especially where she was concerned. 'If something happened to me,' he used to say, 'you'd be provided for.' And, in fact, it is essential to provide for one's needs. But for all the rest, for what is not the most elementary need, how to provide? This is what she felt vaguely, at infrequent intervals. Meanwhile she helped Marcel keep his books and occasionally substituted for him in the shop. Summer was always the hardest, when the heat stifled even the sweet sensation of boredom.

Suddenly, in summer as it happened, the war, Marcel called up then rejected on grounds of health, the scarcity of piece-goods, business at a standstill, the streets empty and hot. If something happened now, she would no longer be provided for. This is why, as soon as piece-goods came back on the market, Marcel had thought of covering the villages of the upper plateaux and of the south himself in order to do without a middleman and sell directly to the Arab merchants. He had wanted to take her along. She knew that travel was difficult, she had trouble breathing, and she would have preferred staying at home. But he was obstinate and she had accepted because it would have taken too much energy to refuse. Here they were and, truly, nothing was like what she had imagined. She had feared the heat, the

swarms of flies, the filthy hotels reeking of aniseed. She
had not thought of the cold, of the biting wind, of these
semi-polar plateaux cluttered with moraines. She had
dreamed too of palm trees and soft sand. Now she saw
that the desert was not that at all, but merely stone,
stone everywhere, in the sky full of nothing but stone-
dust, rasping and cold, as on the ground, where nothing
grew among the stones except dry grasses.

The bus stopped abruptly. The driver shouted a few
words in that language she had heard all her life without ever understanding it. 'What's the matter?' Marcel
asked. The driver, in French this time, said that the sand
must have clogged the carburettor, and again Marcel
cursed this country. The driver laughed hilariously and
asserted that it was nothing, that he would clean the
carburettor and they'd be off again. He opened the
door and the cold wind blew into the bus, lashing their
faces with a myriad grains of sand. All the Arabs silently
plunged their noses into their burnouses and huddled
up. 'Shut the door,' Marcel shouted. The driver laughed
as he came back to the door. Without hurrying, he took
some tools from under the dashboard, then, tiny in
the fog, again disappeared ahead without closing the
door. Marcel sighed. 'You may be sure he's never seen a
motor in his life.' 'Oh, be quiet!' said Janine. Suddenly
she gave a start. On the shoulder of the road close to

the bus, draped forms were standing still. Under the burnous's hood and behind a rampart of veils, only their eyes were visible. Mute, come from nowhere, they were staring at the travellers. 'Shepherds,' Marcel said.

Inside the car there was total silence. All the passengers, heads lowered, seemed to be listening to the voice of the wind loosed across these endless plateaux. Janine was all of a sudden struck by the almost complete absence of luggage. At the end of the railroad line the driver had hoisted their trunk and a few bundles on to the roof. In the racks inside the bus could be seen nothing but gnarled sticks and shopping-baskets. All these people of the South apparently were travelling empty-handed.

But the driver was coming back, still brisk. His eyes alone were laughing above the veils with which he too had masked his face. He announced that they would soon be under way. He closed the door, the wind became silent, and the rain of sand on the windows could be heard better. The motor coughed and died. After having been urged at great length by the starter, it finally sparked and the driver raced it by pressing on the accelerator. With a big hiccough the bus started off. From the ragged clump of shepherds, still motionless, a hand rose and then faded into the fog behind them. Almost at once the vehicle began to bounce on the road, which had become worse. Shaken up, the Arabs constantly swayed. None the less, Janine was feeling overcome with sleep when there suddenly appeared in front of her a little yellow box filled with lozenges. The jackal-soldier was smiling at her. She hesitated, took one, and thanked him. The jackal pocketed the box and simultaneously swallowed his smile. Now he was staring at the road, straight in front of him. Janine turned towards Marcel and saw only the solid back of his neck. Through the window he was watching the denser fog rising from the crumbly embankment.

They had been travelling for hours and fatigue had extinguished all life in the bus when shouts burst forth outside. Children wearing burnouses, whirling like tops, leaping, clapping their hands, were running around the bus. It was now going down a long street lined with low houses; they were entering the oasis. The wind was still blowing, but the walls intercepted the grains of sand which had previously cut off the light. Yet the sky was still cloudy. Amidst shouts, in a great screeching of brakes, the bus stopped in front of the adobe arcades of a hotel with dirty windows. Janine got out and, once on the pavement, staggered. Above the houses she could see a slim yellow minaret. On her left rose the first palm trees of the oasis, and she would have liked to go towards them. But although it was close to noon, the cold was bitter; the wind made her shiver. She turned towards Marcel and saw the soldier coming towards her. She expected him to smile or salute. He passed without looking at her and disappeared. Marcel was busy getting down the trunk of piece-goods, a black foot-locker perched on the bus's roof. It would not be easy. The driver was the only one to take care of the luggage and he had already stopped, standing on the roof, to hold forth to the circle of burnouses gathered around the bus. Janine, surrounded with faces that seemed cut out of bone and leather, besieged by guttural shouts, suddenly became aware of her fatigue. 'I'm going in,' she said to Marcel, who was shouting impatiently at the driver.

She entered the hotel. The manager, a thin, laconic Frenchman, came to meet her. He led her to a second-floor balcony overlooking the street and into a room which seemed to have but an iron bed, a white-enamelled chair, an uncurtained wardrobe, and, behind a rush screen, a washbasin covered with fine sand-dust. When the manager had closed the door, Janine felt the cold coming from the bare, whitewashed walls. She didn't know where to put her bag, where to put herself. She had either to lie down or to remain standing, and to shiver in either case. She remained standing, holding her bag and staring at a sort of window-slit that opened on to the sky near the ceiling. She was waiting, but she didn't know for what. She was aware only of her solitude, and of the penetrating cold, and of a greater weight in the region of her heart. She was in fact dreaming, almost deaf to the sounds rising from the street along with Marcel's vocal outbursts, more aware on the other hand of that sound of a river coming from the window-slit and caused by the wind in the palm trees, so close now, it seemed to her. Then the wind seemed to increase and the gentle ripple of waters became a hissing of waves. She imagined, beyond the walls, a sea of erect, flexible palm trees unfurling in the storm. Nothing was like what she had expected, but those invisible waves refreshed her tired eyes. She was standing, heavy, with dangling arms, slightly stooped, as the cold climbed her thick legs. She was dreaming of the erect and flexible palm trees and of the girl she had once been.

After having washed, they went down to the dining-room. On the bare walls had been painted camels and palm trees drowned in a sticky background of pink and lavender. The arcaded windows let in a meagre light. Marcel questioned the hotel manager about the merchants. Then an elderly Arab wearing a military decoration on his tunic served them. Marcel, preoccupied, tore his bread into little pieces. He kept his wife from drinking water. 'It hasn't been boiled. Take wine.' She didn't like that, for wine made her sleepy. Besides, there was pork on the menu. 'They don't eat it because of the Koran. But the Koran didn't know that well-done pork doesn't cause illness. We French know how to cook. What are you thinking about?' Janine was not thinking of anything, or perhaps of that victory of the cooks over the prophets. But she had to hurry. They were to leave the next morning for still farther south; that afternoon they had to see all the important merchants. Marcel urged the elderly Arab to hurry the coffee. He nodded without smiling and pattered out. 'Slowly in the morning, not too fast in the afternoon,' Marcel said, laughing. Yet eventually the coffee came. They barely took time to swallow it and went out into the dusty, cold street. Marcel called a young Arab to help him carry the trunk, but as a matter of principle quibbled about the payment. His opinion, which he once more expressed to Janine, was in fact based on the vague principle that they always asked for twice as much in the hope of settling for a quarter of the amount. Janine, ill at ease, followed the two trunk-bearers. She had put on a wool dress under her heavy coat and would have liked to take up less space. The pork, although well done, and the small quantity of wine she had drunk also bothered her somewhat.

They walked along a diminutive public garden planted with dusty trees. They encountered Arabs who stepped out of their way without seeming to see them, wrapping themselves in their burnouses. Even when they were wearing rags, she felt they had a look of dignity unknown to the Arabs of her town. Janine followed the trunk, which made a way for her through the crowd. They went through the gate in an earthen rampart and emerged on a little square planted with the same mineral trees and bordered on the far side, where it was widest, with arcades and shops. But they stopped in the square itself in front of a small construction shaped like an artillery shell and painted chalky blue. Inside, in the single room lighted solely by the entrance, an old Arab with a white moustache stood behind a shiny plank. He was serving tea, raising and lowering the teapot over three tiny multi-coloured glasses. Before they could make out anything else in the darkness, the cool scent of mint tea greeted Marcel and Janine at the door. Marcel had barely crossed the threshold and dodged the garlands of pewter teapots, cups and trays, and the postcard displays when he was up against the counter. Janine stayed at the door. She stepped a little aside so as not to cut off the light. At that moment she perceived in the darkness behind the old merchant two Arabs smiling at them, seated on the bulging sacks that filled the back of the shop. Red-and-black rugs and embroidered scarves hung on the walls; the floor was cluttered with sacks and little boxes filled with aromatic seeds. On the counter, beside a sparkling pair of brass scales and an old yardstick with figures effaced, stood a row of loaves of sugar. One of them had been unwrapped from its coarse blue paper and cut into on top. The smell of wool and spices in the room became apparent behind the scent of tea when the old merchant set down the teapot and said good day.

Marcel talked rapidly in the low voice he assumed when talking business. Then he opened the trunk, exhibited the wools and silks, pushed back the scale and yardstick to spread out his merchandise in front of the old merchant. He got excited, raised his voice, laughed nervously, like a woman who wants to make an impression and is not sure of herself. Now, with hands spread wide, he was going through the gestures of selling and buying. The old man shook his head, passed the tea tray to the two Arabs behind him, and said just a few words that seemed to discourage Marcel. He picked up his goods, piled them back into the trunk, then wiped an imaginary sweat from his forehead. He called the little porter and they started off towards the arcades. In the first shop, although the merchant began by exhibiting the same Olympian manner, they were a little luckier.

'They think they're God almighty,' Marcel said, 'but they're in business too! Life is hard for everyone.'

Janine followed without answering. The wind had almost ceased. The sky was clearing in spots. A cold, harsh light came from the deep holes that opened up in the thickness of the clouds. They had now left the square. They were walking in narrow streets along earthen walls over which hung rotted December roses or, from time to time, a pomegranate, dried and wormy. An odour of dust and coffee, the smoke of a wood fire, the smell of stone and of sheep permeated this quarter. The shops, hollowed out of the walls, were far from one another; Janine felt her feet getting heavier. But her husband was gradually becoming more cheerful. He was beginning to sell and was feeling more kindly; he called Janine 'Baby'; the trip would not be wasted. 'Of course,' Janine said mechanically, 'it's better to deal directly with them.'

They came back by another street, towards the centre. It was late in the afternoon; the sky was now almost completely clear. They stopped in the square. Marcel rubbed his hands and looked affectionately at the trunk in front of them. 'Look,' said Janine. From the other end of the square was coming a tall Arab, thin, vigorous, wearing a sky-blue burnous, soft brown boots and gloves and bearing his bronzed aquiline face loftily. Nothing but the *chèche* that he was wearing swathed as a turban distinguished him from those French officers in charge of native affairs whom Janine had occasionally admired. He was advancing steadily towards them, but seemed to be looking beyond their group as he slowly removed the glove from one hand. 'Well,' said Marcel as he shrugged his shoulders, 'there's one who thinks he's a general.' Yes, all of them here had that look of pride; but this one, really, was going too far. Although they were surrounded by the empty space of the square, he was walking straight towards the trunk, without seeing it, without seeing them. Then the distance separating them decreased rapidly and the Arab was upon them when Marcel suddenly seized the handle of the foot-locker and pulled it out of the way. The Arab passed without seeming to notice anything and headed with the same regular step towards the ramparts. Janine looked at her husband; he had his crestfallen look. 'They think they can get away with anything now,' he said. Janine did not reply. She loathed that Arab's stupid arrogance and suddenly felt unhappy. She wanted to leave and thought of her little flat. The idea of going back to the hotel, to that icy room, discouraged her. It suddenly occurred to her that the manager had advised her to climb up to the terrace around the fort to see the desert. She said this to Marcel and that he could leave the trunk at the hotel. But he was tired and wanted to sleep a little before dinner. 'Please,' said Janine. He looked at her, suddenly attentive. 'Of course, my dear,' he said.

She waited for him in the street in front of the hotel. The white-robed crowd was becoming larger and larger. Not a single woman could be seen, and it seemed to Janine that she had never seen so many men. Yet none of them looked at her. Some of them, without appearing to see her, slowly turned towards her that thin, tanned face that made them all look alike to her, the face of the French soldier in the bus and that of the gloved Arab, a face both shrewd and proud. They turned that face towards the foreign woman, they didn't see her, and then, light and silent, they walked around her as she stood there with swelling ankles. And her discomfort, her need of getting away increased. 'Why did I come?' But already Marcel was coming back.

When they climbed the stairs to the fort, it was five o'clock. The wind had died down altogether. The sky, completely clear, was now periwinkle blue. The cold, now drier, made their cheeks smart. Half-way up the stairs an old Arab, stretched out against the wall, asked them if they wanted a guide, but didn't budge, as if he had been sure of their refusal in advance. The stairs were long and steep despite several landings of packed earth. As they climbed, the space widened and they rose into an ever broader light, cold and dry, in which every sound from the oasis reached them pure and distinct. The bright air seemed to vibrate around them with a vibration increasing in length as they advanced, as if their progress struck from the crystal of light a sound-wave that kept spreading out. And as soon as they reached the terrace and their gaze was lost in the vast horizon beyond the palm grove, it seemed to Janine that the whole sky rang with a single short and piercing note, whose echoes gradually filled the space above her, then suddenly died and left her silently facing the limitless expanse.

From east to west, in fact, her gaze swept slowly, without encountering a single obstacle, along a perfect curve. Beneath her, the blue-and-white terraces of the Arab town overlapped one another, splattered with the dark-red spots of peppers drying in the sun. Not a soul could be seen, but from the inner courts, together with the aroma of roasting coffee, there rose laughing voices or incomprehensible stamping of feet. Farther off, the palm grove, divided into uneven squares by clay walls, rustled its upper foliage in a wind that could not be felt up on the terrace. Still farther off and all the way to the horizon extended the ochre-and-grey realm of stones, in which no life was visible. At some distance from the oasis, however, near the wadi that bordered the palm grove on the west could be seen broad black tents. All around them a flock of motionless dromedaries, tiny at that distance, formed against the grey ground the black signs of a strange handwriting, the meaning of which had to be deciphered. Above the desert, the silence was as vast as the space.

Janine, leaning her whole body against the parapet, was speechless, unable to tear herself away from the void opening before her. Beside her, Marcel was getting restless. He was cold; he wanted to go back down. What was there to see here, after all? But she could not take her gaze from the horizon. Over yonder, still farther south, at that point where sky and earth met in a pure line – over yonder it suddenly seemed there was awaiting her something of which, though it had always been lacking, she had never been aware until now. In the advancing afternoon the light relaxed and softened; it was passing from the crystalline to the liquid. Simultaneously, in the heart of a woman brought there by pure chance a knot tightened by the years, habit, and boredom was slowly loosening. She was looking at the nomads' encampment. She had not even seen the men living in it; nothing was stirring among the black tents, and yet she could think only of them whose existence she had barely known until this day. Homeless, cut off from the world, they were a handful wandering over the vast territory she could see, which however was but a paltry part of an even greater expanse whose dizzying course stopped only thousands of miles farther south, where the first river finally waters the forest. Since the beginning of time, on the dry earth of this limitless land scraped to the bone, a few men had been ceaselessly trudging, possessing nothing but serving no one, poverty-stricken but free lords of a strange kingdom. Janine did not know why this thought filled her with such a sweet, vast melancholy that it closed her eyes. She knew that this kingdom had been eternally promised her and yet that it would never be hers, never again, except in this fleeting moment perhaps when she opened her eyes again on the suddenly motionless sky and on its waves of steady light, while the voices rising from the Arab town suddenly fell silent. It seemed to her that the world's course had just stopped and that, from that moment on, no one would ever age any more or die. Everywhere, henceforth, life was suspended – except in her heart, where, at the same moment, someone was weeping with affliction and wonder.

But the light began to move; the sun, clear and devoid of warmth, went down towards the west, which became slightly pink, while a grey wave took shape in the east ready to roll slowly over the vast expanse. A first dog barked and its distant bark rose in the now even colder air. Janine noticed that her teeth were chattering. 'We are catching our death of cold,' Marcel said. 'You're a fool. Let's go back.' But he took her hand awkwardly. Docile now, she turned away from the parapet and followed him. Without moving, the old Arab on the stairs watched them go down towards the town. She walked along without seeing anyone, bent under a tremendous and sudden fatigue, dragging her body, the weight of which now seemed to her unbearable. Her exaltation had left her. Now she felt too tall, too thick, too white too for this world she had just entered. A child, the girl, the dry man, the furtive jackal were the only creatures who could silently walk that earth. What would she do there henceforth except to drag herself towards sleep, towards death?

She dragged herself, in fact, towards the restaurant with a husband suddenly taciturn unless he was telling how tired he was, while she was struggling weakly against a cold, aware of a fever rising within her. Then she dragged herself towards her bed, where Marcel came to join her and put the light out at once without asking anything of her. The room was frigid. Janine felt the cold creeping up while the fever was increasing. She breathed with difficulty, her blood pumped without warming her; a sort of fear grew within her. She turned over and the old iron bedstead groaned under her weight. No, she didn't want to fall ill. Her husband was already asleep; she too had to sleep; it was essential. The muffled sounds of the town reached her through the window-slit. With a nasal twang old phonographs in the Moorish cafés ground out tunes she recognized vaguely; they reached her borne on the sound of a slow-moving crowd. She must sleep. But she was counting black tents; behind her eyelids motionless camels were grazing; immense solitudes were whirling within her. Yes, why had she come? She fell asleep on that question.

She awoke a little later. The silence around her was absolute. But, on the edges of town, hoarse dogs were howling in the soundless night. Janine shivered. She turned over, felt her husband's hard shoulder against hers, and suddenly, half asleep, huddled against him. She was drifting on the surface of sleep without sinking in and she clung to that shoulder with unconscious eagerness as her safest haven. She was talking, but no sound issued from her mouth. She was talking, but she herself hardly heard what she was saying. She could feel only Marcel's warmth. For more than twenty years every night thus, in his warmth, just the two of them, even when ill, even when travelling, as at present . . . Besides, what would she have done alone at home? No child! Wasn't that what she lacked? She didn't know. She simply followed Marcel, pleased to know that someone needed her. The only joy he gave her was the know-ledge that she was necessary. Probably he didn't love her. Love, even when filled with hate, doesn't have that sullen face. But what is his face like? They made love in the dark by feel, without seeing each other. Is there another love than that of darkness, a love that would cry aloud in daylight? She didn't know, but she did know that Marcel needed her and that she needed that need, that she lived on it night and day, at night especially – every night, when he didn't want to be alone, or to age or die, with that set expression he assumed which she occasionally recognized on other men's faces, the only common expression of those madmen hiding under an appearance of wisdom until the madness seizes them and hurls them desperately towards a woman's body to bury in it, without desire, everything terrifying that solitude and night reveals to them.

Marcel stirred as if to move away from her. No, he didn't love her; he was merely afraid of what was not she, and she and he should long ago have separated and slept alone until the end. But who can always sleep alone? Some men do, cut off from others by a vocation or misfortune, who go to bed every night in the same bed as death. Marcel never could do so – he above all, a weak and disarmed child always frightened by suffering,

23

her own child indeed who needed her and who, just at that moment, let out a sort of whimper. She cuddled a little closer and put her hand on his chest. And to herself she called him with the little love-name she had once given him, which they still used from time to time without even thinking of what they were saying.

She called him with all her heart. After all, she too needed him, his strength, his little eccentricities, and she too was afraid of death. 'If I could overcome that fear, I'd be happy . . .' Immediately, a nameless anguish seized her. She drew back from Marcel. No, she was overcoming nothing, she was not happy, she was going to die, in truth, without having been liberated. Her heart pained her; she was stifling under a huge weight that she suddenly discovered she had been dragging about for twenty years. Now she was struggling under it with all her strength. She wanted to be liberated even if Marcel, even if the others, never were! Fully awake, she sat up in bed and listened to a call that seemed very close. But from the edges of night the exhausted and yet indefatigable voices of the dogs of the oasis were all that reached her ears. A slight wind had risen and she heard its light waters flow in the palm grove. It came from the south, where desert and night mingled now under the again unchanging sky, where life stopped, where no one would ever age or die any more. Then the waters of the wind dried up and she was not even sure of having heard anything except a mute call that she could, after all, silence or notice. But never again would she know its meaning unless she responded to it at once. At once – yes, that much was certain at least!

She got up gently and stood motionless beside the bed, listening to her husband's breathing. Marcel was asleep. The next moment, the bed's warmth left her and the cold gripped her. She dressed slowly, feeling for her clothes in the faint light coming through the blinds from the street-lamps. Her shoes in her hand, she reached the door. She waited a moment more in the darkness, then gently opened the door. The knob squeaked and she stood still. Her heart was beating madly. She listened with her body tense and, reassured by the silence, turned her hand a little more. The knob's turning seemed to her interminable. At last she opened the door, slipped outside, and closed the door with the same stealth. Then, with her cheek against the wood, she waited. After a moment she made out, in the distance, Marcel's breathing. She faced about, felt the icy night air against her cheek, and ran the length of the balcony. The outer door was closed. While she was slipping the bolt, the night watchman appeared at the top of the stairs, his face blurred with sleep, and spoke to her in Arabic. 'I'll be back,' said Janine as she stepped out into the night.

Garlands of stars hung down from the black sky over the palm trees and houses. She ran along the short avenue, now empty, that led to the fort. The cold, no longer having to struggle against the sun, had invaded the night; the icy air burned her lungs. But she ran, half blind, in the darkness. At the top of the avenue, however, lights appeared, then descended towards her zigzagging. She stopped, caught the whirr of turning sprockets and, behind the enlarging lights, soon saw vast burnouses surmounting fragile bicycle wheels. The burnouses flapped against her; then three red lights sprang out of the black behind her and disappeared at once. She continued running towards the fort. Half-way up the stairs, the air burned her lungs with such cutting effect that she wanted to stop. A final burst of energy hurled her despite herself on to the terrace, against the parapet, which was now pressing her belly. She was panting and everything was hazy before her eyes. Her running had not warmed her and she was still trembling all over. But the cold air she was gulping down soon flowed evenly inside her and a spark of warmth began to glow amidst her shivers. Her eyes opened at last on the expanse of night.

Not a breath, not a sound – except at intervals the muffled crackling of stones that the cold was reducing to sand – disturbed the solitude and silence surrounding

Janine. After a moment, however, it seemed to her that the sky above her was moving in a sort of slow gyration. In the vast reaches of the dry, cold night, thousands of stars were constantly appearing, and their sparkling icicles, loosened at once, began to slip gradually towards the horizon. Janine could not tear herself away from contemplating those drifting flares. She was turning with them, and the apparently stationary progress little by little identified her with the core of her being, where cold and desire were now vying with each other. Before her the stars were falling one by one and being snuffed out among the stones of the desert, and each time Janine opened a little more to the night. Breathing deeply, she forgot the cold, the dead weight of others, the craziness or stuffiness of life, the long anguish of living and dying. After so many years of mad, aimless fleeing from fear, she had come to a stop at last. At the same time, she seemed to recover her roots and the sap again rose in her body, which had ceased trembling. Her whole belly pressed against the parapet as she strained towards the moving sky; she was merely waiting for her fluttering heart to calm down and establish silence within her. The last stars of the constellations dropped their clusters a little lower on the desert horizon and became still. Then, with unbearable gentleness, the water of night began to fill Janine, drowned the cold, rose gradually from the hidden core of her being and overflowed in wave after wave, rising up even to her mouth full of moans. The next moment, the whole sky stretched out over her, fallen on her back on the cold earth.

When Janine returned to the room, with the same precautions, Marcel was not awake. But he whimpered as she got back in bed and a few seconds later sat up suddenly. He spoke and she didn't understand what he was saying. He got up, turned on the light, which blinded her. He staggered towards the washbasin and drank a long draught from the bottle of mineral water. He was about to slip between the sheets when, one knee on the bed, he looked at her without understanding. She was weeping copiously, unable to restrain herself. 'It's nothing, dear,' she said, 'it's nothing.'

The Silent Men

It was the dead of winter and yet a radiant sun was rising over the already active city. At the end of the jetty, sea and sky fused in a single dazzling light. But Yvars did not see them. He was cycling slowly along the boulevards above the harbour. On the fixed pedal of his cycle his crippled leg rested stiffly while the other laboured to cope with the slippery road surface still wet with the night's moisture. Without raising his head, a slight figure astride the saddle, he avoided the rails of the former tram-line, suddenly turned the handlebars to let cars pass him, and occasionally elbowed back into place the bag in which Fernande had put his lunch. At such moments he would think bitterly of the bag's contents. Between the two slices of coarse bread, instead of the Spanish omelet he liked or the beefsteak fried in oil, there was nothing but cheese.

The ride to the shop had never seemed to him so long. To be sure, he was ageing. At forty, though he had remained as slim as a vine shoot, a man's muscles don't warm up so quickly. At times, reading sports commentaries in which a thirty-year-old athlete was referred to as a veteran, he would shrug his shoulders. 'If he's a veteran,' he would say to Fernande, 'then I'm practically in a wheelchair.' Yet he knew that the reporter wasn't altogether wrong. At thirty a man is already beginning to lose his wind without noticing it. At forty he's not yet in a wheelchair, but he's definitely heading in that direction. Wasn't that just why he now avoided looking towards the sea during the ride to the other end of town where the cooper's shop was? When he was twenty he never got tired of watching it, for it used to hold in store a happy week-end on the beach. Despite or because of his lameness, he had always liked swimming. Then the years had passed, there had been Fernande, the birth of the boy, and, to make ends meet, the overtime, at the shop on Saturdays and on various odd jobs for others on Sundays. Little by little he had lost the habit of those violent days that used to satiate him. The deep, clear water, the hot sun, the girls, the physical life – there was no other form of happiness in this country. And that happiness disappeared with youth. Yvars continued to love the sea, but only at the end of the day when the water in the bay became a little darker. The moment was pleasant on the terrace beside his house where he would sit down after work, grateful for his clean shirt that Fernande ironed so well and for the glass of anisette all frosted over. Evening would fall, the sky would become all soft and mellow, the neighbours talking with Yvars would suddenly lower their voices. At those times he didn't know whether he was happy or felt like crying. At least he felt in harmony at such moments, he had nothing to do but wait quietly, without quite knowing for what.

In the morning when he went back to work, on the other hand, he didn't like to look at the sea. Though it was always there to greet him, he refused to see it until evening. This morning he was pedalling along with head down, feeling even heavier than usual; his heart too was heavy. When he had come back from the meeting, the night before, and had announced that they were going back to work, Fernande had gaily said: 'Then the boss is giving you all a rise?' The boss was not giving any rise; the strike had failed. They hadn't managed things right, it had to be admitted. An impetuous walk-out, and the union had been right to back it up only half-heartedly. After all, some fifteen workers hardly counted; the union had to consider the other cooper's shops that hadn't joined in. You couldn't really blame the union. Cooperage, threatened by the building of tankers and tank trucks, was not thriving. Fewer and fewer barrels and large casks were being made; work consisted chiefly in repairing the huge tuns already in existence. Employers saw their business compromised, to be sure, but even so they wanted to maintain a margin of profit and the easiest way still seemed to them to block wages despite the rise in living costs. What can coopers do when cooperage disappears? You don't change trades when you've gone to the trouble of learning one; this one was hard and called for a long apprenticeship. The good cooper, the one who fits his curved staves and tightens them in the fire with an iron hoop, almost hermetically, without caulking with raffia or oakum, was rare. Yvars knew this and was proud of it. Changing trades is nothing, but to give up what you know, your master-craftsmanship, is not easy. A fine craft without employment and you're stuck, you have to resign yourself. But resignation isn't easy either. It was hard to have one's mouth shut, not to be able to discuss really, and to take the same road every morning with an accumulating fatigue, in order to receive at the end of every week merely what they are willing to give you, which is less and less adequate.

So they had got angry. Two or three of them had hesitated, but the anger had spread to them too after the first discussions with the boss. He had told them flatly, in fact, that they could take it or leave it. A man doesn't talk like that. 'What's he expect of us?' Esposito had said. 'That we'll stoop over and wait to be kicked?' The boss wasn't a bad sort, however. He had inherited from his father, had grown up in the shop, and had known almost all the workers for years. Occasionally he invited them to have a snack in the shop; they would cook sardines or sausage meat over fires of shavings and, thanks partly to the wine, he was really very nice. At New Year he always gave five bottles of vintage wine to each of the men, and often, when one of them was ill or celebrated an event like marriage or first communion, he would make a gift of money. At the birth of his daughter, there had been sugar-coated almonds for everyone. Two or three times he had invited Yvars to shoot on his coastal property. He liked his workmen, no doubt, and often recalled the fact that his father had begun as an apprentice. But he had never gone to their homes; he wasn't aware. He thought only of himself because he knew nothing but himself, and now you could take it or leave it. In other words, he had become obstinate likewise. But, in his position, he could allow himself to be.

He had forced the union's hand, and the shop had closed its doors. 'Don't go to the trouble of picketing,' the boss had said; 'when the shop's not working, I save money.' That wasn't true, but it didn't help matters since he was telling them to their faces that he gave them work out of charity. Esposito was wild with fury and had told him he wasn't a man. The boss was hot-blooded and they had to be separated. But, at the same time, it had made an impression on the workers. Twenty days on strike, the wives sad at home, two or three of them discouraged, and, in the end, the union had advised them to give in on the promise of arbitration and recovery of the lost days through overtime. They had decided to go back to work. Swaggering, of course, and saying that it wasn't all settled, that it would have to be reconsidered. But this morning, with a fatigue that resembled defeat, cheese instead of meat, the illusion was no longer possible. No matter how the sun shone, the sea held forth no more promises. Yvars pressed on his single pedal and with each turn of the wheel it seemed to him he was ageing a little. He couldn't think of the shop, of the fellow workers and the boss he would soon be seeing again without feeling his heart become a trifle heavier. Fernande had been worried: 'What will you men say to him?' 'Nothing,' Yvars had straddled his bicycle, and had shaken his head. He had clenched his teeth; his small, dark, and wrinkled face with its delicate features had become hard. 'We're going back to work. That's enough.' Now he was cycling along, his teeth still clenched, with a sad, dry anger that darkened even the sky itself.

He left the boulevard, and the sea, to attack the moist streets of the old Spanish quarter. They led to an area occupied solely by sheds, junkyards, and garages, where the shop was – a sort of low shed that was faced with stone up to half-way point and then glassed in up to the corrugated metal roof. This shop opened on to the former cooperage, a courtyard surrounded by a covered shed that had been abandoned when the business had enlarged and now served only as a storehouse for worn-out machines and old casks. Beyond the courtyard, separated from it by a sort of path covered with old tiles, the boss's garden began, at the end of which his house stood. Big and ugly, it was nevertheless prepossessing because of the Virginia creeper and the straggling honeysuckle surrounding the outside steps.

Yvars saw at once that the doors of the shop were closed. A group of workmen stood silently in front of them. This was the first time since he had been working here that he had found the doors closed when he arrived. The boss had wanted to emphasize that he had the upper hand. Yvars turned towards the left, parked his bicycle under the lean-to that prolonged the shed on that side, and walked towards the door. From a distance he recognized Esposito, a tall, dark, hairy fellow who worked beside him, Marcou, the union delegate, with his tenor's profile, Saïd, the only Arab in the shop, then

35

all the others who silently watched him approach. But before he had joined them, they all suddenly looked in the direction of the shop doors, which had just begun to open. Ballester, the foreman, appeared in the opening. He opened one of the heavy doors and, turning his back to the workmen, pushed it slowly on its iron rail.

Ballester, who was the oldest of all, disapproved of the strike but had kept silent as soon as Esposito had told him that he was serving the boss's interests. Now he stood near the door, broad and short in his navy-blue jersey, already barefoot (he was the only one besides Saïd who worked barefoot), and he watched them go in one by one with his eyes that were so pale they seemed colourless in his old tanned face, his mouth downcast under his thick, drooping moustache. They were silent, humiliated by this return of the defeated, furious at their own silence, but the more it was prolonged the less capable they were of breaking it. They went in without looking at Ballester, for they knew he was carrying out an order in making them go in like that, and his bitter and downcast look told them what he was thinking. Yvars, for one, looked at him. Ballester, who liked him, nodded his head without saying a word.

Now they were all in the little locker-room on the right of the entrance: open stalls separated by unpainted

boards to which had been attached, on either side, little
locked cupboards; the farthest stall from the entrance,
up against the walls of the shed, had been transformed
into a shower above a gutter hollowed out of the earthen
floor. In the centre of the shop could be seen work
in various stages, already finished large casks, loose-
hooped, waiting for the forcing in the fire, thick benches
with a long slot hollowed out in them (and in some of
them had been slipped circular wooden bottoms waiting to be planed to a sharp edge), and finally cold fires.
Along the wall, on the left of the entrance, the work-
benches extended in a row. In front of them stood piles
of staves to be planed. Against the right wall, not far
from the dressing-room, two large power-saws, thor-
oughly oiled, strong and silent, gleamed.

Some time ago, the workshop had become too big
for the handful of men who worked there. This was an
advantage in the hot season, a disadvantage in winter.
But today, in this vast space, the work dropped half finished, the casks abandoned in every corner with a single
hoop holding the base of the staves spreading at the
top like coarse wooden flowers, the sawdust covering
the benches, the tool-boxes, and machines – everything
gave the shop a look of neglect. They looked at it,
dressed now in their old sweaters and their faded and
patched trousers and they hesitated. Ballester was

watching them. 'So,' he said, 'we get started?' One by one, they went to their posts without saying a word. Ballester went from one to another, briefly reminding them of the work to be begun or finished. No one answered. Soon the first hammer resounded against the iron-tipped wedge sinking a hoop over the convex part of a barrel, a plane groaned as it hit a knot, and one of the saws, started up by Esposito, got under way with a great whirring of blade. Saïd would bring staves on request or light fires of shavings on which the casks were placed to make them swell in their corset of iron hoops. When no one called for him, he stood at a workbench riveting the big rusty hoops with heavy hammer blows. The scent of burning shavings began to fill the shop. Yvars, who was planing and fitting the staves cut out by Esposito, recognized the old scent and his heart relaxed somewhat. All were working in silence, but a warmth, a life was gradually beginning to reawaken in the shop. Through the broad windows a clean, fresh light began to fill the shed. The smoke rose bluish in the golden sunlight; Yvars even heard an insect buzz close to him.

At that moment the door into the former shop opened in the end wall and M. Lassalle, the boss, stopped on the threshold. Thin and dark, he was scarcely more than thirty. His white overall hanging open over a tan gabardine suit, he looked at ease in his body. Despite his very bony face cut like a hatchet, he generally aroused liking, as do most people who exude vitality. Yet he seemed somewhat embarrassed as he came through the door. His greeting was less sonorous than usual; in any case, no one answered it. The sound of the hammers hesitated, lost the beat, and resumed even louder. M. Lassalle took a few hesitant steps, then he headed towards little Valery, who had been working with them for only a year. Near the power-saw, a few feet away from Yvars, he was putting a bottom on a big hogshead and the boss watched him. Valery went on working without saying anything. 'Well, my boy,' said M. Lassalle, 'how are things?' The young man suddenly became more awkward in his movements. He glanced at Esposito, who was close to him, picking up a pile of staves in his huge arms to take them to Yvars. Esposito looked at him too while going on with his work, and Valery peered back into his hogshead without answering the boss. Lassalle, rather nonplussed, remained a moment planted in front of the young man, then he shrugged his shoulders and turned towards Marcou. The latter, astride his bench, was giving the finishing touches, with slow, careful strokes, to sharpening the edge of a bottom. 'Hello, Marcou,' Lassalle said in a flatter voice. Marcou did not answer, entirely occupied with taking very thin shavings off his wood. 'What's got into you?' Lassalle asked in a loud voice as he turned towards the other workmen. 'We didn't agree, to be sure. But that doesn't keep us from having to work together. So what's the use of this?' Marcou got up, raised his bottom piece, verified the circular sharp edge with the palm of his hand, squinted his languorous eyes with a look of satisfaction, and, still silent, went towards another workman who was putting together a hogshead. Throughout the whole shop could be heard nothing but the sound of hammers and of the power-saw. 'OK,' Lassalle said. 'When you get over this, let me know through Ballester.' Calmly, he walked out of the shop.

Almost immediately afterwards, above the din of the shop, a bell rang out twice. Ballester, who had just sat down to roll a cigarette, got up slowly and went to the door at the end. After he had left, the hammers resounded with less noise; one of the workmen had even stopped when Ballester came back. From the door he said merely: 'The boss wants you, Marcou and Yvars.' Yvars's first impulse was to go and wash his hands, but Marcou grasped him by the arm as he went by and Yvars limped out behind him.

Outside in the courtyard, the light was so clear, so liquid, that Yvars felt it on his face and bare arms. They went up the outside stairs, under the honeysuckle on which a few blossoms were already visible. When they entered the corridor, whose walls were covered with diplomas, they heard a child crying and M. Lassalle's voice saying: 'Put her to bed after lunch. We'll call the doctor if she doesn't get over it.' Then the boss appeared suddenly in the corridor and showed them into the little office they already knew, furnished with imitation rustic furniture and its walls decorated with sports trophies. 'Sit down,' Lassalle said as he took his place behind the desk. They remained standing. 'I called you in because you, Marcou, are the delegate and you, Yvars, my oldest employee after Ballester. I don't want to get back to the discussions, which are now over. I cannot, absolutely not, give you what you ask. The matter has been settled, and we reached the conclusion that work had to be resumed. I see that you are angry with me, and that hurts me, I'm telling you just as I feel it. I merely want to add this: what I can't do today I may perhaps be able to do when business picks up. And if I can do it, I'll do it even before you ask me. Meanwhile, let's try to work together.' He stopped talking, seemed to reflect, then looked up at them. 'Well?' he said. Marcou was looking out of the window. Yvars, his teeth clenched, wanted to speak but couldn't. 'Listen,' said Lassalle, 'you have all closed your minds. You'll get over it. But when you become reasonable again, don't forget what I've just said to you.' He rose, went towards Marcou, and held out his hand. 'Ciao!' he said. Marcou suddenly turned pale, his popular tenor's face hardened and, for a second only, became mean-looking. Then he abruptly turned on his heel and went out. Lassalle, likewise pale, looked at Yvars without holding out his hand. 'Go to hell!' he shouted.

When they went back into the shop, the men were lunching. Ballester had gone out. Marcou simply said: 'Just wind,' and returned to his bench. Esposito stopped biting into his bread to ask what they had answered; Yvars said they hadn't answered anything. Then he went to get his haversack and came back and sat down on his workbench. He was beginning to eat when, not far from him, he noticed Saïd lying on his back in a pile of shavings, his eyes looking vaguely at the windows made blue by a sky that had become less luminous. He asked him if he had already finished. Saïd said he had eaten his figs. Yvars stopped eating. The uneasy feeling that hadn't left him since the interview with Lassalle suddenly disappeared to make room for a pleasant warmth. He broke his bread in two as he got up and, faced with Saïd's refusal, said that everything would be better next week. 'Then it'll be your turn to treat me,' he said. Saïd smiled. Now he bit into the piece of Yvars's sandwich, but in a gingerly way like a man who isn't hungry.

Esposito took an old pot and lighted a little fire of shavings and chips. He heated some coffee that he had brought in a bottle. He said it was a gift to the shop that his grocer had made when he learned of the strike's failure. A mustard jar passed from hand to hand. Each time Esposito poured out the already sugared coffee. Saïd swallowed it with more pleasure than he had taken in eating. Esposito drank the rest of the coffee right from the burning pot, smacking his lips and swearing. At that moment Ballester came in to give the back-to-work signal.

While they were rising and gathering papers and utensils into their haversacks, Ballester came and stood in their midst and said suddenly that it was hard for all, and for him too, but that this was no reason to act like children and that there was no use in sulking. Esposito, the pot in his hand, turned towards him; his long, coarse face had suddenly become flushed. Yvars knew what he was about to say – and what everyone was thinking at the same time – that they were not sulking, that their mouths had been closed, they had to take it or leave it, and that anger and helplessness sometimes hurt so much that you can't even cry out. They were men, after all, and they weren't going to begin smiling and simpering. But Esposito said none of this, his face finally relaxed, and he slapped Ballester's shoulder gently while the others went back to their work. Again the hammers rang out, the big shed filled with the familiar din, with the smell of shavings and of old clothes damp with sweat. The big saw whined and bit into the fresh wood of the stave that Esposito was slowly pushing in front of him. Where the saw bit, damp sawdust spurted out and covered, with something like bread-crumbs, the big hairy hands firmly gripping the wood on each side of the moaning blade. Once the stave was ripped, you could hear only the sound of the motor.

At present Yvars felt only the strain in his back as he leaned over the plane. Generally the fatigue didn't come until later on. He had got out of training during these weeks of inactivity, it was clear. But he thought also of age, which makes manual labour harder when it's not mere precision work. That strain also foreshadowed old age. Wherever the muscles are involved, work eventually becomes hateful, it precedes death, and on evenings following great physical effort sleep itself is like death. The boy wanted to become a schoolteacher, he was right; those who indulge in clichés about manual work don't know what they're talking about.

When Yvars straightened up to catch his breath and also to drive away these evil thoughts, the bell rang out again. It was insistent, but in such a strange way, with stops and imperious starts, that the men interrupted their work. Ballester listened, surprised, then made up his mind and went slowly to the door. He had disappeared for several seconds when the ringing finally ceased. They resumed work. Again the door was flung open and Ballester ran towards the locker-room. He came out wearing canvas shoes and, slipping on his jacket, said to Yvars as he went by: 'The child has had an attack. I'm off to get Germain,' and he ran towards the main door. Dr Germain took care of the shop's health; he lived in this outlying quarter. Yvars repeated the news without commentary. They gathered around him and looked at one another, embarrassed. Nothing could be heard but the motor of the power-saw running freely. 'It's perhaps nothing,' one of them said. They went back to their places, the shop filled again with their noises, but they were working slowly, as if waiting for something.

A quarter of an hour later, Ballester came in again, hung up his jacket, and, without saying a word, went out through the little door. On the windows the light was getting dimmer. A little later, in the intervals when the saw was not ripping into the wood, the dull bell of an ambulance could be heard, at first in the distance, then nearer, finally just outside. Then silence. After a moment Ballester came back and everyone went up to him. Esposito had turned off the motor. Ballester said

45

that while undressing in her room the child had suddenly keeled over as if mowed down. 'Did you ever hear
anything like it!' Marcou said. Ballester shook his head
and gestured vaguely towards the shop; but he looked
as if he had had quite a turn. Again the ambulance bell
was heard. They were all there, in the silent shop, under
the yellow light coming through the glass panels, with
their rough, useless hands hanging down along their
old sawdust-covered trousers.

The rest of the afternoon dragged. Yvars now felt
only his fatigue and his still heavy heart. He would have
liked to talk. But he had nothing to say, nor had the
others. On their uncommunicative faces could be read
merely sorrow and a sort of obstinacy. Sometimes the
word 'calamity' took shape in him, but just barely, for it
disappeared immediately – as a bubble forms and bursts
simultaneously. He wanted to get home, to be with
Fernande again, and the boy, on the terrace. As it happened, Ballester announced closing-time. The machines
stopped. Without hurrying, they began to put out the
fires and to put everything in order on their benches,
then they went one by one to the locker-room. Saïd
remained behind; he was to clean up the shop and water
down the dusty soil. When Yvars reached the locker-
room, Esposito, huge and hairy, was already under the
shower. His back was turned to them as he soaped

himself noisily. Generally, they kidded him about his modesty; the big bear, indeed, obstinately hid his pudenda. But no one seemed to notice on this occasion. Esposito backed out of the shower and wrapped a towel around him like a loincloth. The others took their turns, and Marcou was vigorously slapping his bare sides when they heard the big door roll slowly open on its cast-iron wheel. Lassalle came in.

He was dressed as at the time of his first visit, but his hair was rather dishevelled. He stopped on the threshold, looked at the vast deserted shop, took a few steps, stopped again, and looked towards the locker-room. Esposito, still covered with his loincloth, turned towards him. Naked, embarrassed, he teetered from one foot to the other. Yvars thought that it was up to Marcou to say something. But Marcou remained invisible behind the sheet of water that surrounded him. Esposito grabbed a shirt and was nimbly slipping it on when Lassalle said: 'Good night,' in a rather toneless voice and began to walk towards the little door. When it occurred to Yvars that someone ought to call him, the door had already closed.

Yvars dressed without washing, said good night likewise, but with his whole heart, and they answered with the same warmth. He went out rapidly, got his bicycle, and, when he straddled it, he felt the strain in his back again. He was cycling along now in the late afternoon through the trafficky city. He was going fast because he was eager to get back to the old house and the terrace. He would wash in the washhouse before sitting down to look at the sea, which was already accompanying him, darker than in the morning, above the parapet of the boulevard. But the little girl accompanied him too and he couldn't stop thinking of her.

At home, his boy was back from school and reading the picture papers. Fernande asked Yvars whether everything had gone all right. He said nothing, cleaned up in the washhouse, then sat down on the bench against the low wall of the terrace. Mended washing hung above his head and the sky was becoming transparent; over the wall the soft evening sea was visible. Fernande brought the anisette, two glasses, and the jug of cool water. She sat down beside her husband. He told her everything, holding her hand as in the early days of their marriage. When he had finished, he didn't stir, looking towards the sea where already, from one end of the horizon to the other, the twilight was swiftly falling. 'Ah! it's his own fault!' he said. If only he were young again, and Fernande too, they would have gone away, across the sea.

The Guest

The schoolmaster was watching the two men climb towards him. One was on horseback, the other on foot. They had not yet tackled the abrupt rise leading to the schoolhouse built on the hillside. They were toiling onwards, making slow progress in the snow, among the stones, on the vast expanse of the high, deserted plateau. From time to time the horse stumbled. Without hearing anything yet, he could see the breath issuing from the horse's nostrils. One of the men, at least, knew the region. They were following the trail although it had disappeared days ago under a layer of dirty white snow. The schoolmaster calculated that it would take them half an hour to get on to the hill. It was cold; he went back into the school to get a sweater.

He crossed the empty, frigid classroom. On the blackboard the four rivers of France, drawn with four different coloured chalks, had been flowing towards their estuaries for the past three days. Snow had suddenly fallen in mid October after eight months of drought without the transition of rain, and the twenty pupils, more or less, who lived in the villages scattered over the plateau had stopped coming. With fair weather they would return. Daru now heated only the single room that was his lodging, adjoining the classroom and giving also on to the plateau to the east. Like the class windows, his window looked to the south too. On that side the school was a few kilometres from the point where the plateau began to slope towards the south. In clear weather could be seen the purple mass of the mountain range where the gap opened on to the desert.

Somewhat warmed, Daru returned to the window from which he had first seen the two men. They were no longer visible. Hence they must have tackled the rise. The sky was not so dark, for the snow had stopped falling during the night. The morning had opened with a dirty light which had scarcely become brighter as the ceiling of clouds lifted. At two in the afternoon it seemed as if the day were merely beginning. But still this was better than those three days when the thick snow was falling amidst unbroken darkness with little gusts of wind that rattled the double door of the classroom. Then Daru had spent long hours in his room, leaving it only to go to the shed and feed the chickens or get some coal. Fortunately the delivery truck from

Tadjid, the nearest village to the north, had brought his supplies two days before the blizzard. It would return in forty-eight hours.

Besides, he had enough to resist a siege, for the little room was cluttered with bags of wheat that the administration left as a stock to distribute to those of his pupils whose families had suffered from the drought. Actually they had all been victims because they were all poor. Every day Daru would distribute a ration to the children. They had missed it, he knew, during these bad days. Possibly one of the fathers or big brothers would come this afternoon and he could supply them with grain. It was just a matter of carrying them over to the next harvest. Now shiploads of wheat were arriving from France and the worst was over. But it would be hard to forget that poverty, that army of ragged ghosts wandering in the sunlight, the plateaux burned to a cinder month after month, the earth shrivelled up little by little, literally scorched, every stone bursting into dust under one's foot. The sheep had died then by thousands and even a few men, here and there, sometimes without anyone's knowing.

In contrast with such poverty, he who lived almost like a monk in his remote schoolhouse, none the less satisfied with the little he had and with the rough life, had felt like a lord with his whitewashed walls, his narrow couch, his unpainted shelves, his well, and his weekly provision of water and food. And suddenly this snow, without warning, without the foretaste of rain. This is the way the region was, cruel to live in, even without men – who didn't help matters either. But Daru had been born here. Everywhere else, he felt exiled.

He stepped out on to the terrace in front of the schoolhouse. The two men were now half-way up the slope. He recognized the horseman as Balducci, the old gendarme he had known for a long time. Balducci was holding on the end of a rope an Arab who was walking behind him with hands bound and head lowered. The gendarme waved a greeting to which Daru did not reply, lost as he was in contemplation of the Arab dressed in a faded blue jellaba, his feet in sandals but covered with socks of heavy raw wool, his head surmounted by a narrow, short *chèche*. They were approaching. Balducci was holding back his horse in order not to hurt the Arab, and the group was advancing slowly.

Within earshot, Balducci shouted: 'One hour to do the three kilometres from El Ameur!' Daru did not answer. Short and square in his thick sweater, he watched them climb. Not once had the Arab raised his head. 'Hello,' said Daru when they got up on to the terrace. 'Come in and warm up.' Balducci painfully got down from his horse without letting go the rope. From under his bristling moustache he smiled at the school-master. His little dark eyes, deep-set under a tanned forehead, and his mouth surrounded with wrinkles made him look attentive and studious. Daru took the bridle, led the horse to the shed, and came back to the two men, who were now waiting for him in the school. He led them into his room. 'I am going to heat up the classroom,' he said. 'We'll be more comfortable there.' When he entered the room again, Balducci was on the couch. He had undone the rope tying him to the Arab, who had squatted near the stove. His hands still bound, the *chèche* pushed back on his head, he was looking towards the window. At first Daru noticed only his huge lips, fat, smooth, almost negroid; yet his nose was straight, his eyes were dark and full of fever. The *chèche* revealed an obstinate forehead and, under the weath-ered skin now rather discoloured by the cold, the whole face had a restless and rebellious look that struck Daru when the Arab, turning his face towards him, looked him straight in the eyes. 'Go into the other room,' said the schoolmaster, 'and I'll make you some mint tea.' 'Thanks,' Balducci said. 'What a nuisance! How I long for retirement.' And addressing his prisoner in Arabic: 'Come on, you.' The Arab got up and, slowly, holding his bound wrists in front of him, went into the class-room.

With the tea, Daru brought a chair. But Balducci was already enthroned on the nearest pupil's desk and the Arab had squatted against the teacher's platform facing the stove, which stood between the desk and the window. When he held out the glass of tea to the prisoner, Daru hesitated at the sight of his bound hands. 'He might perhaps be untied.' 'Certainly,' said Balducci. 'That was for the journey.' He started to get to his feet. But Daru, setting the glass on the floor, had knelt beside the Arab. Without saying anything, the Arab watched him with his feverish eyes. Once his hands were free, he rubbed his swollen wrists against each other, took the glass of tea, and sucked up the burning liquid in swift little sips.

'Good,' said Daru. 'And where are you headed for?'

Balducci withdrew his moustache from the tea. 'Here, my boy.'

'Odd pupils! And you're spending the night?'

'No. I'm going back to El Ameur. And you will deliver this fellow to Tinguit. He is expected at police headquarters.'

Balducci was looking at Daru with a friendly little smile.

'What's this story?' asked the schoolmaster. 'Are you pulling my leg?'

'No, my boy. Those are the orders.'

'The orders? I'm not . . .' Daru hesitated, not wanting to hurt the old Corsican. 'I mean, that's not my job.'

'What! What's the meaning of that? In wartime people do all kinds of jobs.'

'Then I'll wait for the declaration of war!'

Balducci nodded.

'OK. But the orders exist and they concern you too. Things are brewing, it appears. There is talk of a forthcoming revolt. We are mobilized, in a way.'

Daru still had his obstinate look.

'Listen, my boy,' Balducci said. 'I like you and you must understand. There's only a dozen of us at El Ameur to patrol throughout the whole territory of a small department and I must get back in a hurry. I was told to hand this man over to you and return without delay. He couldn't be kept there. His village was beginning to stir; they wanted to take him back. You must take him to Tinguit tomorrow before the day is over. Twenty kilometres shouldn't worry a husky fellow like you. After that, all will be over. You'll come back to your pupils and your comfortable life.'

Behind the wall the horse could be heard snorting and pawing the earth. Daru was looking out of the window. Decidedly, the weather was clearing and the light was increasing over the snowy plateau. When all the snow was melted, the sun would take over again and once more would burn the fields of stone. For days, still, the unchanging sky would shed its dry light on the solitary expanse where nothing had any connexion with man.

'After all,' he said, turning around towards Balducci, 'what did he do?' And, before the gendarme had opened his mouth, he asked: 'Does he speak French?'

'No, not a word. We had been looking for him for a month, but they were hiding him. He killed his cousin.'

'Is he against us?'

'I don't think so. But you can never be sure.'

'Why did he kill?'

'A family squabble, I think. One owed the other grain, it seems. It's not at all clear. In short, he killed his cousin with a billhook. You know, like a sheep, *kreezk*!'

Balducci made the gesture of drawing a blade across his throat and the Arab, his attention attracted, watched him with a sort of anxiety. Daru felt a sudden wrath against the man, against all men with their rotten spite, their tireless hates, their blood lust.

But the kettle was singing on the stove. He served Balducci more tea, hesitated, then served the Arab again, who, a second time, drank avidly. His raised arms made the jellaba fall open and the schoolmaster saw his thin, muscular chest.

'Thanks, my boy,' Balducci said. 'And now, I'm off.'

He got up and went towards the Arab, taking a small rope from his pocket.

'What are you doing?' Daru asked dryly.

Balducci, disconcerted, showed him the rope.

'Don't bother.'

The old gendarme hesitated. 'It's up to you. Of course, you are armed?'

'I have my shotgun.'

'Where?'

'In the trunk.'

'You ought to have it near your bed.'

'Why? I have nothing to fear.'

'You're mad. If there's an uprising, no one is safe, we're all in the same boat.'

'I'll defend myself. I'll have time to see them coming.'

Balducci began to laugh, then suddenly the moustache covered the white teeth.

'You'll have time? OK. That's just what I was saying. You have always been a little cracked. That's why I like you, my son was like that.'

At the same time he took out his revolver and put it on the desk.

'Keep it; I don't need two weapons from here to El Ameur.'

The revolver shone against the black paint of the

table. When the gendarme turned towards him, the schoolmaster caught the smell of leather and horse-flesh.

'Listen, Balducci,' Daru said suddenly, 'every bit of this disgusts me, and most of all your fellow here. But I won't hand him over. Fight, yes, if I have to. But not that.'

The old gendarme stood in front of him and looked at him severely.

'You're being a fool,' he said slowly. 'I don't like it either. You don't get used to putting a rope on a man even after years of it, and you're even ashamed – yes, ashamed. But you can't let them have their way.'

'I won't hand him over,' Daru said again.

'It's an order, my boy, and I repeat it.'

'That's right. Repeat to them what I've said to you: I won't hand him over.'

Balducci made a visible effort to reflect. He looked at the Arab and at Daru. At last he decided.

'No, I won't tell them anything. If you want to drop us, go ahead; I'll not denounce you. I have an order to deliver the prisoner and I'm doing so. And now you'll just sign this paper for me.'

'There's no need. I'll not deny that you left him with me.'

'Don't be mean with me. I know you'll tell the truth.

You're from hereabouts and you are a man. But you must sign, that's the rule.'

Daru opened his drawer, took out a little square bottle of purple ink, the red wooden penholder with the 'sergeant-major' pen he used for making models of penmanship, and signed. The gendarme carefully folded the paper and put it into his wallet. Then he moved towards the door.

'I'll see you off,' Daru said.

'No,' said Balducci. 'There's no use being polite. You insulted me.'

He looked at the Arab, motionless in the same spot, sniffed peevishly, and turned away towards the door. 'Goodbye, son,' he said. The door shut behind him. Balducci appeared suddenly outside the window and then disappeared. His footsteps were muffled by the snow. The horse stirred on the other side of the wall and several chickens fluttered in fright. A moment later Balducci reappeared outside the window leading the horse by the bridle. He walked towards the little rise without turning round and disappeared from sight with the horse following him. A big stone could be heard bouncing down. Daru walked back towards the prisoner, who, without stirring, never took his eyes off him. 'Wait,' the schoolmaster said in Arabic and went towards the bedroom. As he was going through the door, he had a second thought, went to the desk, took the revolver, and stuck it in his pocket. Then, without looking back, he went into his room.

For some time he lay on his couch watching the sky gradually close over, listening to the silence. It was this silence that had seemed painful to him during the first days here, after the war. He had requested a post in the little town at the base of the foothills separating the upper plateaux from the desert. There, rocky walls, green and black to the north, pink and lavender to the south, marked the frontier of eternal summer. He had been named to a post farther north, on the plateau itself. In the beginning, the solitude and the silence had been hard for him on these wastelands peopled only by stones. Occasionally, furrows suggested cultivation, but they had been dug to uncover a certain kind of stone good for building. The only ploughing here was to harvest rocks. Elsewhere a thin layer of soil accumulated in the hollows would be scraped out to enrich paltry village gardens. This is the way it was: bare rock covered three-quarters of the region. Towns sprang up, flourished, then disappeared; men came by, loved one another or fought bitterly, then died. No one in this desert, neither he nor his guest, mattered. And yet, outside this desert neither of them, Daru knew, could have really lived.

When he got up, no noise came from the classroom. He was amazed at the unmixed joy he derived from the mere thought that the Arab might have fled and that he would be alone with no decision to make. But the prisoner was there. He had merely stretched out between the stove and the desk. With eyes open, he was staring at the ceiling. In that position, his thick lips were particularly noticeable, giving him a pouting look. 'Come,' said Daru. The Arab got up and followed him. In the bedroom, the schoolmaster pointed to a chair near the table under the window. The Arab sat down without taking his eyes off Daru.

'Are you hungry?'

'Yes,' the prisoner said.

Daru set the table for two. He took flour and oil, shaped a cake in a frying-pan, and lighted the little stove that functioned on bottled gas. While the cake was cooking, he went out to the shed to get cheese, eggs, dates, and condensed milk. When the cake was done he set it on the window sill to cool, heated some condensed milk diluted with water, and beat up the eggs into an omelet. In one of his motions he knocked against the revolver stuck in his right pocket. He set the bowl down, went into the classroom, and put the revolver in his desk drawer. When he came back to the room, night was falling. He put on the light and served the Arab. 'Eat,' he said. The Arab took a piece of the cake, lifted it eagerly to his mouth, and stopped short.

'And you?' he asked.

'After you. I'll eat too.'

The thick lips opened slightly. The Arab hesitated, then bit into the cake determinedly.

The meal over, the Arab looked at the schoolmaster. 'Are you the judge?'

'No, I'm simply keeping you until tomorrow.'

'Why do you eat with me?'

'I'm hungry.'

The Arab fell silent. Daru got up and went out. He brought back a folding bed from the shed, set it up between the table and the stove, at right-angles to his own bed. From a large suitcase which, upright in a corner, served as a shelf for papers, he took two blankets and arranged them on the camp bed. Then he stopped, felt useless, and sat down on his bed. There was nothing more to do or to get ready. He had to look at this man. He looked at him, therefore, trying to imagine his face bursting with rage. He couldn't do so. He could see nothing but the dark yet shining eyes and the animal mouth.

'Why did you kill him?' he asked in a voice whose hostile tone surprised him.

The Arab looked away.

'He ran away. I ran after him.'

He raised his eyes to Daru again and they were full of a sort of woeful interrogation. 'Now what will they do to me?'

'Are you afraid?'

He stiffened, turning his eyes away.

'Are you sorry?'

The Arab stared at him open-mouthed. Obviously he did not understand. Daru's annoyance was growing. At the same time he felt awkward and self-conscious with his big body wedged between the two beds.

'Lie down there,' he said impatiently. 'That's your bed.'

The Arab didn't move. He called to Daru:

'Tell me!'

The schoolmaster looked at him.

'Is the gendarme coming back tomorrow?'

'I don't know.'

'Are you coming with us?'

'I don't know. Why?'

The prisoner got up and stretched out on top of the blankets, his feet towards the window. The light from the electric bulb shone straight into his eyes and he closed them at once.

'Why?' Daru repeated, standing beside the bed.

The Arab opened his eyes under the blinding light and looked at him, trying not to blink.

'Come with us,' he said.

In the middle of the night, Daru was still not asleep. He had gone to bed after undressing completely; he generally slept naked. But, when he suddenly realized that he had nothing on, he hesitated. He felt vulnerable and the temptation came to him to put on his clothes again. Then he shrugged his shoulders; after all, he wasn't a child and, if need be, he could break his adversary in two. From his bed he could observe him, lying on his back, still motionless with his eyes closed under the harsh light. When Daru turned out the light, the darkness seemed to coagulate all of a sudden. Little by little, the night came back to life in the window where the starless sky was stirring gently. The schoolmaster soon made out the body lying at his feet. The Arab still did not move, but his eyes seemed open. A faint wind was prowling around the schoolhouse. Perhaps it would drive away the clouds and the sun would reappear.

During the night the wind increased. The hens fluttered a little and then were silent. The Arab turned over on his side with his back to Daru, who thought he heard him moan. Then he listened for his guest's breathing become heavier and more regular. He listened to that breath so close to him and mused without being able to go to sleep. In this room where he had been sleeping alone for a year, this presence bothered him. But it bothered him also by imposing on him a sort of brotherhood he knew well but refused to accept in the present circumstances. Men who share the same rooms, soldiers or prisoners, develop a strange alliance as if, having cast off their armour with their clothing, they fraternized every evening, over and above their differences, in the ancient community of dream and fatigue. But Daru shook himself; he didn't like such musings, and it was essential to sleep.

A little later, however, when the Arab stirred slightly, the schoolmaster was still not asleep. When the prisoner made a second move, he stiffened, on the alert. The Arab was lifting himself slowly on his arms with almost the motion of a sleepwalker. Seated upright in bed, he waited motionless without turning his head towards Daru, as if he were listening attentively. Daru did not stir; it had just occurred to him that the revolver was still in the drawer of his desk. It was better to act at once. Yet he continued to observe the prisoner, who, with the same slithery motion, put his feet on the ground, waited again, then began to stand up slowly. Daru was about to call out to him when the Arab began to walk, in a quite natural but extraordinarily silent way. He was heading towards the door at the end of the room that opened into the shed. He lifted the latch with precaution and went out, pushing the door behind him but without shutting it. Daru had not stirred. 'He is running away,' he merely thought. 'Good riddance!' Yet he listened attentively. The hens were not fluttering; the guest must be on the plateau. A faint sound of water reached him, and he didn't know what it was until the Arab again stood framed in the doorway, closed the door carefully, and came back to bed without a sound. Then Daru turned his back on him and fell asleep. Still later he seemed, from the depths of his sleep, to hear furtive steps around the schoolhouse. 'I'm dreaming! I'm dreaming!' he repeated to himself. And he went on sleeping.

When he awoke, the sky was clear; the loose window let in a cold, pure air. The Arab was asleep, hunched up under the blankets now, his mouth open, utterly relaxed. But when Daru shook him, he started dreadfully, staring at Daru with wild eyes as if he had never seen him and such a frightened expression that the schoolmaster stepped back. 'Don't be afraid. It's me. You must eat.' The Arab nodded his head and said yes. Calm had returned to his face, but his expression was vacant and listless.

The coffee was ready. They drank it seated together on the folding bed as they munched their pieces of the cake. Then Daru led the Arab under the shed and showed him the tap where he washed. He went back into the room, folded the blankets and the bed, made his own bed and put the room in order. Then he went through the classroom and out on to the terrace. The sun was already rising in the blue sky; a soft, bright light was bathing the deserted plateau. On the ridge the snow was melting in spots. The stones were about to reappear. Crouched on the edge of the plateau, the schoolmaster looked at the deserted expanse. He thought of Balducci. He had hurt him, for he had sent him off in a way as if he didn't want to be associated with him. He could still hear the gendarme's farewell and, without knowing why, he felt strangely empty and vulnerable. At that moment, from the other side of the schoolhouse, the prisoner coughed. Daru listened to him almost despite himself and then, furious, threw a pebble that whistled through the air before sinking into the snow. That man's stupid crime revolted him, but to hand him over was contrary to honour. Merely thinking of it made him smart with humiliation. And he cursed at one and the same time his own people who had sent him this Arab and the Arab too who had dared to kill and not managed to get away. Daru got up, walked in a circle on the terrace, waited motionless, and then went back into the schoolhouse.

The Arab, leaning over the cement floor of the shed, was washing his teeth with two fingers. Daru looked at him and said: 'Come.' He went back into the room ahead of the prisoner. He slipped a hunting-jacket on over his sweater and put on walking-shoes. Standing, he waited until the Arab had put on his *chèche* and sandals. They went into the classroom and the schoolmaster pointed to the exit, saying: 'Go ahead.' The fellow didn't budge. 'I'm coming,' said Daru. The Arab went out. Daru went back into the room and made a package of pieces of rusk, dates, and sugar. In the classroom, before going out, he hesitated a second in front of his desk, then crossed the threshold and locked the door. 'That's the way,' he said. He started towards the east, followed by the prisoner. But, a short distance from the schoolhouse, he thought he heard a slight sound behind them. He retraced his steps and examined the surroundings of the house; there was no one there. The Arab watched him without seeming to understand. 'Come on,' said Daru.

They walked for an hour and rested beside a sharp peak of limestone. The snow was melting faster and faster and the sun was drinking up the puddles at once, rapidly cleaning the plateau, which gradually dried and vibrated like the air itself. When they resumed walking, the ground rang under their feet. From time to time a bird rent the space in front of them with a joyful cry.

Daru breathed in deeply the fresh morning light. He felt a sort of rapture before the vast familiar expanse, now almost entirely yellow under its dome of blue sky. They walked an hour more, descending towards the south. They reached a level height made up of crumbly rocks. From there on, the plateau sloped down, eastward, towards a low plain where there were a few spindly trees and, to the south, towards outcroppings of rock that gave the landscape a chaotic look.

Daru surveyed the two directions. There was nothing but the sky on the horizon. Not a man could be seen. He turned towards the Arab, who was looking at him blankly. Daru held out the package to him. 'Take it,' he said. 'There are dates, bread, and sugar. You can hold out for two days. Here are a thousand francs too.' The Arab took the package and the money but kept his full hands at chest level as if he didn't know what to do with what was being given him. 'Now look,' the schoolmaster said as he pointed in the direction of the east, 'there's the way to Tinguit. You have a two-hour walk. At Tinguit you'll find the administration and the police. They are expecting you.' The Arab looked towards the east, still holding the package and the money against his chest. Daru took his elbow and turned him rather roughly towards the south. At the foot of the height on which they stood could be seen a faint path. 'That's the trail across the plateau. In a day's walk from here you'll find pasture lands and the first nomads. They'll take you in and shelter you according to their law.' The Arab had now turned towards Daru and a sort of panic was visible in his expression. 'Listen,' he said. Daru shook his head: 'No, be quiet. Now I'm leaving you.' He turned his back on him, took two long steps in the direction of the school, looked hesitantly at the motionless Arab, and started off again. For a few minutes he heard nothing but his own step resounding on the cold ground and did not turn his head. A moment later, however, he turned around. The Arab was still there on the edge of the hill, his arms hanging now, and he was looking at the schoolmaster. Daru felt something rise in his throat. But he swore with impatience, waved vaguely, and started off again. He had already gone some distance when he again stopped and looked. There was no longer anyone on the hill.

Daru hesitated. The sun was now rather high in the sky and was beginning to beat down on his head. The schoolmaster retraced his steps, at first somewhat uncertainly, then with decision. When he reached the little hill, he was bathed in sweat. He climbed it as fast as he could and stopped, out of breath, at the top. The rock-fields to the south stood out sharply against the blue sky, but on the plain to the east a steamy heat was already rising. And in that slight haze, Daru, with heavy heart, made out the Arab walking slowly on the road to prison.

A little later, standing before the window of the classroom, the schoolmaster was watching the clear light bathing the whole surface of the plateau, but he hardly saw it. Behind him on the blackboard, among the winding French rivers, sprawled the clumsily chalked-up words he had just read: 'You handed over our brother. You will pay for this.' Daru looked at the sky, the plateau, and, beyond, the invisible lands stretching all the way to the sea. In this vast landscape he had loved so much, he was alone.

RYŪNOSUKE AKUTAGAWA *Hell Screen*

KINGSLEY AMIS *Dear Illusion*

SAUL BELLOW *Him With His Foot in His Mouth*

DONALD BARTHELME *Some of Us Had Been Threatening Our Friend Colby*

SAMUEL BECKETT *The Expelled*

JORGE LUIS BORGES *The Widow Ching – Pirate*

PAUL BOWLES *The Delicate Prey*

ITALO CALVINO *The Queen's Necklace*

ALBERT CAMUS *The Adulterous Woman*

TRUMAN CAPOTE *Children on Their Birthdays*

ANGELA CARTER *Bluebeard*

RAYMOND CHANDLER *Killer in the Rain*

EILEEN CHANG *Red Rose, White Rose*

G. K. CHESTERTON *The Strange Crime of John Boulnois*

JOSEPH CONRAD *Youth*

ROBERT COOVER *Romance of the Thin Man and the Fat Lady*

ISAK DINESEN *Babette's Feast*

MARGARET DRABBLE *The Gifts of War*

HANS FALLADA *Short Treatise on the Joys of Morphinism*

F. SCOTT FITZGERALD *Babylon Revisited*

IAN FLEMING *The Living Daylights*

E. M. FORSTER *The Machine Stops*

SHIRLEY JACKSON *The Tooth*

HENRY JAMES *The Beast in the Jungle*

M. R. JAMES *Canon Alberic's Scrap-Book*

JAMES JOYCE *Two Gallants*

FRANZ KAFKA *In the Penal Colony*

RUDYARD KIPLING *'They'*

D. H. LAWRENCE *Odour of Chrysanthemums*

PRIMO LEVI *The Magic Paint*

H. P. LOVECRAFT *The Colour Out Of Space*

MALCOLM LOWRY *Lunar Caustic*

CARSON MCCULLERS *Wunderkind*

KATHERINE MANSFIELD *Bliss*

ROBERT MUSIL *Flypaper*

VLADIMIR NABOKOV *Terra Incognita*

R. K. NARAYAN *A Breath of Lucifer*

FRANK O'CONNOR *The Cornet-Player Who Betrayed Ireland*

DOROTHY PARKER *The Sexes*

LUDMILLA PETRUSHEVSKAYA *Through the Wall*

JEAN RHYS *La Grosse Fifi*

SAKI *Filboid Studge, the Story of a Mouse That Helped*

ISAAC BASHEVIS SINGER *The Last Demon*

WILLIAM TREVOR *The Mark-2 Wife*

JOHN UPDIKE *Rich in Russia*

H. G. WELLS *The Door in the Wall*

EUDORA WELTY *Moon Lake*

P. G. WODEHOUSE *The Crime Wave at Blandings*

VIRGINIA WOOLF *The Lady in the Looking-Glass*

STEFAN ZWEIG *Chess*

a little history

Penguin Modern Classics were launched in 1961, and have been shaping the reading habits of generations ever since.

The list began with distinctive grey spines and evocative pictorial covers – a look that, after various incarnations, continues to influence their current design – and with books that are still considered landmark classics today.

Penguin Modern Classics have caused scandal and political change, inspired great films and broken down barriers, whether social, sexual or the boundaries of language itself. They remain the most provocative, groundbreaking, exciting and revolutionary works of the last 100 years (or so).

In 2011, on the fiftieth anniversary of the Modern Classics, we're publishing fifty Mini Modern Classics: the very best short fiction by writers ranging from Beckett to Conrad, Nabokov to Saki, Updike to Wodehouse. Though they don't take long to read, they'll stay with you long after you turn the final page.

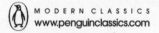 MODERN CLASSICS
www.penguinclassics.com